TRIG

BY

ROBERT NEWTON PECK

Illustrated by Pamela Johnson

A Yearling Book

Published by
Dell Publishing Co., Inc.
1 Dag Hammarskjold Plaza
New York, New York 10017

Yearling ® TM 913705, Dell Publishing Co., Inc.

ISBN: 0-440-49098-7

Reprinted by arrangement with Little, Brown and Company
Printed in the United States of America
First Yearling printing—August 1979

CW

To my mother,
one of the best rifle shots
in the county.

A QUICK LOOK AT ELIZABETH
BEFORE HER STORY BEGINS

BY THE WAY THAT I WAS FLYING up in the air and over the barn, just by flapping my arms like a crow, I knew it was only a dumb old dream.

Over my eyes, instead of my steamy-up glasses that my mother says I have to wear, I now wore yellow goggles. And a yellow aviator's helmet to match my yellow polka-dot nightgown. Even dreaming, I could still sort of feel the muslin of my pillow rub under my cheek (scrubbing off a few freckles, I hope) and only the sheet around my shoulder, as it was a hot summer night.

Sure was fun to fly!

Only last Sunday, I still had on my church dress when we all hurried over to Mister Doogree's pasture to see a *real* honest-to-gosh aviator. While we stood around in the heat and waited and waited and waited for Christmas, I heard Miss Millerton say that today would mark the first time that an airplane ever landed in our town. Somebody said he hoped the pilot could get the plane down. That was when Vestal McEvoy spat out his tobacco to say that, according to what little he'd heard about flying machines, "they *all* come down. Question is . . . *how?*"

"Here it comes!" a kid shouted.

Sure enough, we spotted a speck coming our way. We were all looking straight up, and as the airplane circled and circled, I thought my neck would ache off.

Hoover Peacham's wife said to her husband, "I'd hate to be up there in *that* thing."

Hoover, in his usual slow voice, said, "Well, I'd hate to be up there without it."

Minute by minute, more cars and more wagons arrived in the dust; until the whole State of Vermont, or darn near, turned out to see the airplane show. All the plane did

was circle and cough, like a hawk with the croup. As we all stood around Mister Doogree's meadow, squinting at the sun, Marvin Fillput, who clerks at the feed store, stepped smack into the middle of a cowflop. And with his good Sunday shoes. Mister Fillput didn't say anything, looking up. Later on, when he finally got around to looking down at his feet, he sure said a few things. Not what you'd call Sunday words either. More like Saturday night; and as Mama was standing behind me, she put her hands over my ears. I was glad she did it too late.

From then on that afternoon, seeing as I am only half as tall as grown-ups, I had more fun watching Marvin Fillput watch out for his other shoe, instead of straining my chin to see a dumb old triplane duck in and out of the clouds. And every darn fool pointing when it was in plain sight. It was fun when the rain finally come, all of a sudden, to shoo us all under a canopy of big elm trees. Until the thunder struck, which flushed us all out again.

They told me the name of that famous cropduster fellow who was the pilot of the flying machine, like he was sort of a hero or something. But I wasn't in the market for another hero, not when I already nailed a picture of Bill Dickey over my bed. Bill was catcher for the New York Yankees.

I didn't need a airplane either. Somewhere in the crowd, I could still hear Marvin Fillput telling people about his step in the wrong direction, as if it was the biggest thing that ever happened. Life sure must be dull at the feed store.

I drifted back into my dream again, and looking down from where I was, high in the sky and still flying with just my arms, I

could see our red barn and all our white chickens no bigger than snowflakes. Out by the front veranda, I spotted Mama, about the size of an ant and near as nervous, shouting up to me:

"Elizabeth, come down!"

Her voice was faint and far off, as she was waving her yellow apron to warn me that best I not fly loopity-loops so close to our barn in my yellow polkadot nightie, because I was still only a kid in pigtails. But I knew better than to crash into the hencoop or the milkhouse or anything; because when you fly in a dream, I don't guess you ever crack yourself up. Or down. Another thing, when you sink into water that's away over your head in a dream, you hold your breath until heck won't have it. Leastwise, I usual do. Until you sort of know it's only a dream and then puff like an uphill horse.

So, even though I was falling a bit, I put my arms around my pillow and around Fred, my doll, to let myself fall frisky and feel all the fun out of it. Mud splattered all over my nightgown when I finally went splooshing down in the middle of a puddle in our pigsty. One good thing about mud in a dream; nobody ever points at you or hands you heck for getting so dirty. My mud just sort of melted away as simple as smoke.

Over the fence I scampered, ahead of Mortimer.

He's our big old boar-hog and he can be about as tart as spring cider. To be honest, I can't own up to recalling exactly what spring cider tastes like, on account that I am seldom allowed to share any whenever the menfolk pull the bung and draw off a jack. You can't draw off ripe applejack from a keg of sweet cider until you get a long freeze, I heard a guy say. Not until there's ice in the barrel. Ferment the fall and freeze the winter. Then what you drain off the spout is what *don't* freeze. They call it Jack on account it kicks like a male ass. Once when nobody was looking, I sampled a sip from Cousin Noble's cup. One hot swallow was sure enough. It was hardly what you'd call a taste. For a breath or two, and longer, I felt as if I'd ate a hacksaw.

Later on the same evening that I'd sneaked a sip, I took notice that Cousin Noble was singing kind of sour. He sure walked off-key, too, when they stood him up on his feet. Then out on the side porch, which is under my bedroom window where I can listen down and hear new words, Noble missed his footing and toppled over like a wet rag into Mama's rose hedge. Fell laughing, and landed crying. Small wonder, as there must be easy a thousand thorns in that hedge. Leastwise, *used* to be. Reckon now that a good share of those old prickers found a new home in Cousin Noble.

He stopped singing.

The whole crash made me ponder if rose needles were as mean and mifty as spring cider, or applejack, and meaner than Mortimer our boar-hog. Well, nothing or nobody could act as ornery as either Bud Griffin or Skip Warner, the two boys that live downroad from us Trigmans. I sure would cotton to pick a scrap with those two birds, I was dreaming to myself; and on *my* side I get Mortimer. And before the fight, I'd measure out Mortimer a snort of spring cider to really irk his ire.

Back at the pigsty I heard a grunt, so I hunkered down to a look-see through the bars, and there was big Mortimer's mean old eyes staring right back at me, which was enough to make me turkey thankful that our old boar was at the *in* of the fence and I was shut out. But I imagined for a moment that he sort of smiled and winked his pink eye at me; I don't guess that old Mortimer ever before seen me in my yellow polkadot nightie. With goggles to match.

I rolled over in bed.

The sun was just fixing to climb the east hill. Papa always said that we were so lucky to live right here in Vermont instead of New Hampshire; on account that away over east of us, the sun hits there first and all the farm folks abed have to get up earlier. Well, I was thinking as I opened my eyes and yawned and stretched one leg and then the other like Romeo our tomcat, we're lucky not to have to farm it over in New Hampshire, because morning chores come plenty early here to home, in Vermont.

"Elizabeth!"

I heard Mama's voice and this time it was real as breakfast. Time to get up and race the sun to the henhouse. It took me a minute to kick my feet into my green sneakers and pull a dress over my head, and hook on my glasses. Before coming to the table it was my job to collect the eggs and rag off the specks. One brown egg was wet from laying and still smelled of hen. Then I ran down to the barnyard to slide open the gate-bars to let our herd into the barn for milk-ing. Except in cold weather, our Holsteins all get turned out to meadowland both day and night. But come morning and evening milk-time, we always let each old girl come

into the barn, and right to her own stanchion.

Like usual, Boots was the first cow to come see me. She was mostly white, but black from her knees down, so I named her Boots. She let out a friendly beller to say good morning, and to hurry up. Right after I shot open the bars, old Joppa was first through, as always. No other cow would have the gumption to set hoof in front of *her*. Not even Sheba, our biggest milker. Like it was some sort of law, Joppa always entered the barn first. And left first. Joppa was wise as wisdom, Papa once said, as she seemed to always know where the clover was sweet and the crick-water cool. She was our bellcow, and yet she didn't even need a clanker bell tied around her neck to prove it. All our cows know that Joppa's their queen.

Like at school.

Miss Millerton is boss, and it's meet with

me; on account of when *she* puts a yard-stick to Bud Griffin or Skip, they doggone well know who rules the roost. Not that Miss Millerton favors Joppa in looks or anything like that. After all, one's a Holstein and one's a Methodist. Even so, both Joppa and Miss Millerton have nice eyes, brown and soft, and they sort of look right through your soul if you're tardy for either chores or school.

Boots is still my favorite cow.

She's only three years old. I raised her from a heifer. Once I stayed with Boots almost all night long in the barn when she dropped her first calf. So maybe that's why Boots is willing to be the last cow in line, into the barn and to her proper stanchion, because I walk beside her every step of the way. My green sneakers look a mite puny next to her heavy hoofs, but I don't guess that Boots pays much of a nevermind to sizes. After I click the stanchion bars around her neck, for milking and to keep the cows in a row, sometimes I whisper a secret to her, giving her ears and neck a scratch as I do. Boots likes it whenever I do that. Then I hug her some, to let her know that she is still my calf; and my baby, even though she must weigh over a thousand pounds, easy. All I weigh is 57.

"Good morning, Boots. Sleep well?"

My cow didn't say a word. If'n she had I reckon I'd a run for the kitchen.

Hearing the clink-clank of silver milk-pails, I turned around to see Papa smile my way. He nudged the hickory milkstool with his boot before kneeling down under Joppa. Before milking, he ragged off her udder real proper, so's all her creamy bubbles wouldn't be all peppered with grit. Next to my father, Stephen Farnum, a highschool boy who helps with the milking, set his silver pail under Sheba.

Joppa is my father's favorite cow.

Not that he ever told me so. I just know. As he milked her, his head bowed forward, almost as though he was saying a little prayer, with his brow resting on her warm flank. Joppa was mostly black, but the place on her right side where Papa leaned his head was a white star, no bigger than his

hand. It was his milking pillow; and he let
his head rest on her soft white star, morning
and evening. To see him do it each morn
always seemed to say that Vermont had
rolled up her sleeves, our workday had
started, and life was in line. Like our cows.

Then I listened to the music of the milk,
as the thin white ribbons began to ring the
two empty pails, like churchbells. With my
face pressed to a cow's warm neck, I heard
the chimes of choretime.

"Boots," I whispered, "we hatched our-
selves a new day."

TRIG

"BEAT IT, Elizabeth. Go on home."

Bud Griffin gave my shoulder a push as he said it. Maybe he expected me to trip over Skip Warner, the chubby creep with sort of white curly hair, who had crept up behind me, down on his elbows and knees, to make me take a backward spill and rip my dress. Instead of falling, I sat down on the back of Skip's dirty neck, real hard, to duck his fat face into the dirt.

"I want to play," I said.

"Now scram, Elizabeth," said Bud. "You're too small to play Cops and Robbers."

"And you're a *girl*," said Skip. The grit on his broad nose and cheek made me a bit happier, but not a whole lot.

"Okay," I said to Fat Face, which was my name for Skip, "so I'm a girl."

"Dumb old girls can't play Cops and Robbers."

"Well, if you ask me," I said to Bud Griffin, "you're no cop." And then to Skip I said, "and you're no robber. You two guys are just kids, like me."

"Scram," said Bud. "I got red hair, Elizabeth, so don't get me mad." He was standing with his feet apart and his fists rested on the hips of his faded blue overalls. He was wearing a shirt over his overall straps, but I could see that, even though Bud was skinnier than Skip, his arms and shoulders were thicker than mine. I was glad his sunburn was peeling and I hoped it itched like heck.

Skip was only a year older than I was, and Bud was a year older than Skip, but both boys thought they were real big onions.

Bud and Skip were both barefoot. As their toes looked so mean and dirty, I remembered how hard they could kick. Standing there, I was angry at my mother for making me wear my green sneakers on such a hot July morning. Just what you might expect from someone who named me Elizabeth when there were plenty of nifty names around, like Skip or Bud.

So I left.

But not before I stuck my tongue out

and made my loudest and most disgusting noise. The one I'm sort of famous for. Just thinking about Skip and his fake Tom Mix six-shooter made me kick a cowflop.

I hate myself and I hate my name, I was thinking as I trudged up the pasture path to our farmhouse. Who wants to be Elizabeth Trigman? I sure don't.

That was the day I got my gun.

When I got home, there was Uncle Fred's bright yellow Model-T-Ford. His real and righteous name was Fredrick McDonald, so my mother and father call him Mac sometimes, just for short. But even though he

was Mama's brother, they said I wasn't allowed to call him Mac. Isn't that just like grown-ups? So I was supposed to call him Uncle Fred. Well, it was jake with me. Having my Uncle Fred for an uncle almost made it worth being Elizabeth.

My green sneakers busted into a gallop. As I hurdled the fence, my knee scraped as I landed on the gravel but no matter.

The only grudge I had against Uncle Fred was that when he came to visit us, he brought his darn wife. Mama said I was to call her Aunt Augusta even though *she* was no relation. Thank gosh, as I'd sooner be niece to a toad. It was a hot day for running, but Uncle Fred didn't mind the sweaty bearhug I gave him. He kissed my hurt knee. One of my green sneakers was loose, like always, and Uncle Fred tied it soon as I jumped up on his lap.

"Hi ya, Mac," I whispered in his ear, making him grin.

"Your *church* suit," Aunt Augusta said to Uncle Fred, to warn a clean uncle not to touch a dirty kid.

Augusta was too heavy, Mama said once, and she sported too much rouge and lipstick, and too much jewelry. Her bracelets rattled whenever she was talking which was usual always. Mama even said to Papa once, when she thought I was asleep, that Aunt Augusta likes to gussy-up like a "circus horse." After that, I asked Aunt Augusta if she really *was* in a circus . . . and then Mama had a cough spell when she hadn't even took sick.

"For *you*," Uncle Fred's finger poked me in the ribs to make me giggle, "I brung a sweet surprise!"

"What?"

"It's out in the Ford."

"A *catcher's* mitt?" I jumped off his lap so fast my glasses almost fell off. Probable would have, except that I got real big ears.

At least so Aunt Augusta told me when she caught me listening in on some of their dumb old grown-up talk, about somebody *going* with somebody. They never do say *where*.

"Better'n that," smiled Uncle Fred.

"A cowgirl lasso? A tommy gun? Shin guards? Just like Bill Dickey's?" I had his picture over my bed, and I couldn't fall asleep unless I kissed Bill goodnight. Sure wouldn't be easy to kiss a man with a catcher's mask over his face, which made me sort of feel sorry for Mrs. Dickey.

"Wait'll you see," winked Uncle Fred.

It took near to a hundred years to walk to the Ford, on account that Uncle Fred whistled, picked a buttercup, and listened to a robin sing in our maple tree, like he had nothing on his mind. Or in his car. He sure knew how to get my goat. Another century ticked by as he pulled off a million sheets of brown wrapping paper.

"A machine gun!" I screamed.

It was big as a cannon! Stood on end, it was longer than I was tall. But I could lift it. Uncle Fred put my right hand on the trigger and tried to stretch my left to the handle grip in front of a thing halfway along that looked like a giant hockey puck. "Where the bullets go," Uncle Fred said with a wink.

"Real bullets?"

"Well, sort of. I'll bring the pretend bullets next trip."

"True and honest?"

"Cross my heart," said Uncle Fred, "and hope to turn blue and throw up breakfast." He sure knew a lot of neat stuff to say.

"Thank you, Uncle Fred." The gun made me sort of forget about calling him Mac. I kissed his cheek just like with Bill Dickey. "This here's my first gun, and it's even better than my doll."

"Pet," he said, pulling one of my pigtails,

"about that Shirley Temple doll we brung ya last Christmas . . ."

"I like the doll. I named her Fred, after you. Best doll I ever got. Honest."

"You're the best niece I ever got."

He stopped pulling my pigtail. His big hand touched my face, sort of the way you'd stroke a kitten or a frog you liked a whole darn lot, and wiped my glasses clear with the fresh part of his hanky.

"Better?"

I nodded. I wanted to ask Uncle Fred why he and Aunt Augusta didn't get busy and have a little girl of their own. But I'd got told by Mama never to ask that question. I'd already asked it once at the supper table, and it sure made everybody stop talking.

"You got more pollywogs on your nose." Uncle Fred never called them freckles. He pretended to count 'em all up.

"Sure do. Uncle Fred, what kind of a gun is this?"

"This here," his rough hand patted the big brown stock, "is a . . . see here, it's writ on the barrel . . . a genuine Melvin Purvis official Junior G-man machine gun."

I sighed, not wanting to break the spell with mere words, as it would have been an indignity to Mr. Melvin Purvis, who was the most fearless peace officer in the entire forty-eight states in the U.S. of A. At least everybody here in Vermont talked about him whenever his name come over the radio. He was a G-man, the head one. And I figured he had a nickname, too, like Mel or maybe Pur.

"Melvin Purvis," said Uncle Fred looking serious, "is a pal o' mine, and this here gun is the very weapon he used to bag that famous bank robber, John Dillinger."

"Honest injun?"

Uncle Fred winked and nodded. "You betcha. Now, ya see this here lever? Well, to cock it, ya pull her back." Making about a hundred clicks, the spring, or whatever it was inside, stretched and I felt like a big bomb was fixing to explode. "Now," he said, "pull the trigger."

Closing my eyes, using three fingers, I pulled.

BBRRATTAT-TAT-TAT-TAT.

My ears near to busted. Uncle Fred hung on to me real tight, or I'd a gone trunk-over-teakettle.

"What a kick," I said. "Like it's alive."

We heard talk from the house, adult voices that might be fixing to disapprove of Junior G-man guns, and even of Mr. Purvis. They probable figured that Uncle Fred's car made that loud noise, like it usual did. So I'd let 'em think so. In a quick, Uncle Fred cocked the gun again for me, slapped my rump, and said "Scat! And don't display that gun at the house until you hear my old flivver crank up and scoot for Burlington."

"Check," I said, throwing Uncle Fred a salute.

"Now git."

I could've used the stile, but I'm sort of preferenced to climbing. Going over the fence, and then hauling my new gun gently through the crossbars, I come up with another of my plentiful great ideas. This one was one *bang* of a brainstorm. I didn't have to be Elizabeth Trigman anymore. Well, I did; but not every darn minute. If old Purvis is Pur (or Mel) and Fredrick McDonald boils down to just plain Mac, then you just know what that makes me:

"Trigman is Trig," I said out loud. "Trig."

Wow, what a name! It's got a real zonk to it. Trig, I said over and over to myself as I walked along on the pasture grass. Trig, Trig, Trig; and it sounded sort of like "pig, pig, pig, here pig, pig, pig (like when you slop 'em) but I didn't give a goat's butt. At

32

least I was somebody. I was Trig. Thank
you, Mel, and thank you, Mac.

A few minutes later I was away down
meadow, just this side of the crick, trying
to decide what to shoot at. I sort of hoped
that somebody like John Dillinger or Al
Capone would come along so I could *really*
be Melvin Purvis, which for now was even
more fun than being Bill Dickey. I tippy-
toed along the slippery wet pebbles until
both my green sneakers were soaked. Then
I headed up pasture, for higher ground,
where I could draw a bead on John or Al, or
maybe just one of our cows.

What I sighted was two boys, fishing. So

with no handy gangster for a target, I'd just have to make do with good old Bud and Skip.

Their backs were to me, and they were talking, like always. Boys and their big mouths. If any boy could scrap as well as jabber, he'd lick the whole State of Vermont, I reckon. No chance of that. Sneaking up real close, I wiped my glasses on the hem of my dress (making 'em dirtier), so I could get the two gangsters clear in my sights. I was hoping they'd skinny off their overalls and jump in the crick for a swim, so I could sneak up and tie knots in their pantlegs. Anything to get even. Well, for now I'd content myself to *scare* 'em both out of their britches. My new Junior G-man gun would make such a fuss and fury that I was too tense to pull the trigger.

And before I could, they turned around and spotted me. My heart fell and broke like it busted clear through. I muffed it.

The chance of my life slipped through my fingers and went *thud*. I darn near cried, and would have, but for the fact I had just cleaned my glasses. Not saying a word, I walked right up to where they stood, closed my ears, and squeezed the trigger.

BBRRAATT-AT-TAT-TAT.

Bud Griffin and Skip Warner always told me how much gumption they both had, and nothing living or dead could ever spook them. Nothing except a machine gun. Stepping backward, their bare feet slipped on the grassy bank and the next sound I heard was a pretty pair of ker-splashes. Both of 'em, clothes and all, were soaking wet and sputtering like Bud swallowed half the crick and Skip the other.

"What in the name of Sam Hill is that contraption?" asked Skip.

Bud's question was next. "What . . . what *is* it?"

"Don't you goofs know what this is?"

They climbed up and out, soaked through. But it was a hot day so I didn't waste a pity. Not on that pair.

"Stand back," I said, "as there ain't much that's more dangerous than a genuine Melvin Purvis official Junior G-man machine gun."

Bud and Skip couldn't even say "mud." They just stood there, all a-drip, staring at my new gun with their mouths open. Dumb boys.

"Is it yours?"

"Bet your bellybutton," I said.

"Hey," said Bud, "can I see it, Elizabeth?"

"First off," I said, "there's going to be a few changes made around here, and I'm the one that's fixing to make 'em."

"Like what?" asked Skip.

"Well," I said, "it's high time we formed a gang of Junior G-men around these parts, now that we got the proper gun."

"Yeah," said Skip, like it was his idea.

"And I'm the *boss*," I said, holding my breath.

"Sure thing, Elizabeth."

"Another thing," I said, making myself spit, "you don't call your boss Elizabeth. My name is Miss Trigman, but for short, you two and the rest of our gang can just call me Trig."

"Uh . . . sure thing, Trig."

"What are we going to do?" asked Bud.

"I been studying that. And one thing we're going to do," I said, "is shoot somebody."

"Who we gonna shoot, Trig?"

"Somebody bad," I said.

"Who?"

"You'll see. First thing we do," I said, setting down the gun as it was growing more than a mite heavy, "is draw a plan of the hideout, just like G-men always do."

"Whose hideout?"

"*Their* hideout," I said, "They're the bad guys and we're the good."

"You ain't a guy," said Skip. "You're a . . ."

"Trig is anybody she wants," said Bud to Skip who just stood there scratching himself. And then Bud rested his hand on my shoulder like I was his pal. Usually when he did that, he did it a lot harder and I always bit his thumb. But not this time.

"Right," I said. "Skip, you gotta quit scratching. You'll rub yourself raw."

"But I itch."

"Yeah?" I said. "Well, you don't see Mr. Melvin Purvis scratch *his* butt all the time, do ya, and let old Dillinger get away?"

"Reckon not."

"Okay," I said, "here's the plan. This here tree stump is the bank robbers' hide-out, and these pebbles is the three of us. We'll move in slow and easy." I kicked each little stone with the toe of my sneaker.

"Who totes the gun?" asked Bud.

It felt like he was fixing to lift his hand off my shoulder. But I figured he might ask that question, so I was more than ready with an answer. "You," I said, smiling at Bud. However, the real and righteous reason I was smiling was because I had a plan to get even with just about everybody and not even get caught. Trig, I told myself, you got one beaut of a brain.

"How come *him*?" asked Skip.

"On account of you scratch so much," I said, "you'd like to drop the gun, so it'll go off by accident and kill us all."

"Kill us?"

"Well, wound us maybe," said Bud.

"You don't wound criminals or cops," I said.

"What do ya do?" Bud asked me.

"You wing 'em."

Bud picked up the gun. "Careful," I said. After I spoke he carried that gun like you bring home eggs. As we walked up pasture, I didn't really know who we'd shoot. But I sure was all a-bubble with one heck of a hope. We just sort of headed toward my house. "That's the hideout!" I yelled, and even though it was a hot day, all three of us busted into a run. From under the cool shade of a meadow elm, several black and white milkcows watched us as we raced by, the way only a cow can look at a fool. You sure don't need much sense to run on a July afternoon. Near to the house, I spotted Aunt Augusta, who looked to be sound asleep in our backyard hammock.

"Hot spit," I just had to say.

"Now what, Trig?"

"We work in," I said, "close as courting."

"Who is it?" asked the boys in a whisper.

"That," I said, pointing with the finger that had my best nail, "is our target, better known by us Junior G-men as Public Enemy Number One, although she goes by lots of Alices."

"What's an Alice?" whispered Bud.

"It's a new word," I explained, "that I spotted in the paper last week, something about a desperate ex-con who don't always use his real name. Instead he uses an Alice."

"A man uses an *Alice*?"

I nodded. "Hush now, or we'll wake up Augusta."

"Hey," whispered Skip, "I thought you said her name was Alice?"

"Well, it sort of is. Let's go." I didn't want to bother answering such a dumb old question. Or explain about Mr. Capone and that Al was maybe short for Alice. Least, not to Fat Face.

Crawling on our bellies, through the grass just north of the cowbarn, we moved quietly. I could even hear the crick water slosh around inside my sneakers. We advanced until the three of us were darn near to under where Aunt Augusta, feet up and shoes off, made one heck of a big bulge in our hammock. She filled the canvas like a breeze to a frigate. We were so close I could even see a tiny hole in the toe of Aunt Augusta's stocking. It took all three of us to cock the gun.

"Trig?" whispered Bud.

"Yeah."

"You sure this Alice can take a joke?"

"Yep," I said, "she'll take it." I neglected to say how. "Just pretend you're Melvin Purvis and that she's John Dillinger."

"You mean," said Bud, "You'll let *me* shoot her?"

My get-even plan was working. "Sure," I said in my bighearted voice. "In fact, you and Skip can *both* hold the gun, so she won't kick up."

"Wow!" Skip's appreciating was near to a prayer.

"Okay, you men. Move in and open fire."

As the two boys crept forward, I could see how dirty the soles of their feet were. Those twenty toes sure were equal strangers to soap and water. Holding my breath, I saw Skip and Bud point the gun at Aunt Augusta, almost touching her. I backed up, hid in the grass, covered my ears and shut my eyes. Even so, my heart near to stopped when I heard it.

BBBRRAAATAT-TAT-TAT-TAT.

Something made me open my eyes, and I was sure glad I did, for what went on next was a sight I sure would've hated to miss.

Hammocks act up sort of funny at times, like they got a skittery nature all to their own. If you lie in one, best you keep your balance, as a bed's got four legs but a hammock's got nary a one. Least little thing can flop it over. So when Aunt Augusta's entire and enormous body went rigid as if she'd been shocked with over a zillion volts of electricity, the hammock seemed to react by tossing her like a skillet can turn a pancake. Aunt Augusta flipped like a flapjack.

Down she come on Skip and Bud. And a good half of Vermont shook like an earthquake when she landed, so I sure didn't envy my two pals. Then out came words I never figured Augusta knew. She sure had the temper of a wet cat. She grabbed Skip and Bud by the hair, knocking their heads together so hard it made my teeth hurt. I

laughed; but as the boys were yelling for
help so loud, nobody heard me.

"You young hellions," panted Aunt
Augusta, shaking the unholy bejeepers out
of the two boys.

Then my heart almost stopped!

Her face purple with rage, Aunt Augusta
made a grab for my beautiful machine gun.

Oh no. She'd smash it for sure. Augusta pulled, her hammy hands holding the barrel, but Skip and Bud held on to their end. Skip still gripped the trigger ring and

Bud took a firm purchase on the cocking lever and it looked to me as if both were too scared to let loose. As my Aunt Augusta gave the gun a stout yank, I saw the gun cock. I even heard the click click click of the spring. And then somehow Aunt Augusta gained control of the gun; and even though she was in her stocking feet, she turned her ankle. She did that a lot. But I always thought it was because, as Mama always said, she wore her heels higher than decent.

Her right thumb, however, stuck itself in the ring around the trigger, and the tip of the gun barrel wedged into the bracelets around her left wrist. Both her hands spread out like a big bird; but what was funniest was that my machine was behind her back, sort of out of her sight.

BBBRRRAAATTT-TAT-TAT-TAT-TAT-TAT.

Aunt Augusta squeezed off the longest burst of the day, turning her around and

around, as that gun had a heck of a back-
fire. Around she went, screaming, until she
tripped over the hammock, again landing
on Skip and Bud. Must've hurt like hives.
Lying on top of those two boys, her stocking feet kicked the air higher than a branded
calf. As she rolled off I heard Skip, or Bud,
grunt with relief.

Their faces white, eyes popped open,
they crawled toward me on their hands and
knees. "Alice is nuts," said Bud, and I
thought I'd giggle fit to bust. And in the
same breath, I was gosh grateful it weren't
me that got so busted.

Having heard the screams and the BRAT-
TAT-TAT of my machine gun (which was
now sort of Aunt Augusta's machine gun),
Mama came out of the house, wiping her
hands on her apron, and with a wonder-
ing look on her face.

"My thumb!" shrieked Aunt Augusta,
struggling to her feet. Her thumb was stuck

for sure in the trigger hole, and now it was one heck of a swollen item.

"Hold still, Augusta," said Mama, "and I'll try to turn you loose. That is if I can get a purchase on that gadget."

Aunt Augusta had no intention of standing still. But she should have. Looking down at her feet, I saw a hornet on the grass. Like lots of folks, and cows, the hornet was sort of drowsy from the heat of the day and seemed too lazy to move. And as Aunt Augusta stepped on him in her stocking feet, I wondered if that old brown hornet was too lazy to sting.

He wasn't.

"Yeeeeooowww!" yelled Aunt Augusta.

She danced around some. From the expression on my mother's face, I could tell that Mama didn't know about the hornet. She told Aunt Augusta to please hold her horses and she'd yank her thumb out of the trigger. So my aunt held still for a moment, which turned out to be another grave error. Her feet were still, too.

And that was when the hornet decided to hunt a hideout of his own. So he just crawled into a handy hole, the very hole in the toe of my Aunt Augusta's stocking.

"Yipes!" yelled Augusta. She wiggled her chubby toes and, my hunch was, gave the hornet a stout pinch.

"What is it?" asked Mama.

"A *bee*!"

"No," I said, "it's a hornet," which made Skip and Bud, who were lying in the grass on either side of me, snicker.

"It's crawling up my *leg*!" screamed Aunt Augusta, hopping around, her hands still wide apart. She had become quite attached to my machine gun.

"I don't see any hornet," said Mama.

"Ahhh! Inside my stocking!" cried Aunt

Augusta, her voice (as well as the hornet) climbing higher.

Uncle Fred came out of the house. One of his hands held the weekly paper, and the other scratched his head. "What are you two girls up to?" He looked half asleep, and yet I could've took an oath his face was smiling a mite.

Augusta didn't answer. She screamed. Ted Rafferty told me once that you don't never holler at a hornet, on account of it sort of nerves it up. Well, it seemed right then that Aunt Augusta's hornet was more than a bit highstrung. Ted Rafferty also said that a hornet ain't like a bee that stings just once. Hornets sting again and again, and it sure seemed to be the straight of it, as I watched Aunt Augusta prance around.

Her thumb was still wedged in the trigger ring, but she worked her other hand free. Ted Rafferty never told me the best way to swat a hornet. Aunt Augusta's way was to whack her own leg with a Melvin Purvis official Junior G-man machine gun. Whack by whack, I could see that my aunt felt the target crawl higher. The hornet seemed to work around back and up inside her undies.

Her face was now as purple as her thumb. Purpler.

"Trig," said Bud, "I ain't seen so much fun since my pa caught his tie in the toaster."

"Me neither, Trig," said Skip.

I'd never seen nobody catch a necktie in a toaster, so I asked Bud a question. "Will he ever do it again so I can watch?"

"Naw, after his tie busted into flame all the way up to his Adam's apple, he tried to throw the toaster out the back door."

"How far'd he throw it?"

"Not very far. It was still plugged in, so it kind of whipped around his neck a couple of turns. You know, like a yo-yo."

My smile hurt, I was laughing so hard. So was Skip.

"Did it put out the fire?"

"No. His tie was still burning so Ma throwed a dipper of water on him. The water must've dunked in the toaster, which was still plugged to the socket, 'cause you should a' seen the electric show Pa put on for us. It blew out all the lights in the house, except for the sparks from the toaster. A regular Fourth of July, and Ma said he'd toasted everything except the bread."

My sides was split open from giggling,

and my eyes cried so bad that my glasses were all wet and I couldn't see. Sure was fun. "Stop, stop," I was trying to say, but couldn't quit laughing enough to even get it out. I thought for sure I'd rip a rib.

About an hour later, we got Aunt Augusta calmed down. And the hornet calmed down. Off he flew. It took soap and a screwdriver to work her thumb loose of my machine gun. Aunt Augusta moaned a good bit, but didn't talk much, which gave all our ears a breather. Uncle Fred said so long and promised me a catcher's mitt on the next trip. I darn near asked him to bring pretend bullets but I don't guess it'd been too keen a question. He and Augusta drove off.

For the rest of the day until almost chore time, Skip and Bud hung around to play Cops and Robbers and I was the boss. We ran around some. After my Aunt Augusta lands on folks they limp a lot, so Bud and Skip couldn't catch me and my green sneakers. But my mother sure caught those two boys, by the hair, and gave 'em one scat of a scolding for bringing *their* awful gun to our house and scaring people.

They tried to say it was *my* gun, the old squealers, which made Mama tell them that a young lady like *her* Elizabeth did *not* play with machine guns, and *not* to tell fibs. I don't guess I ever tried harder to choke back a giggle, watching Mama hold those boys by the hair. She wasn't very gentle. Later, when she wasn't looking, I hid my gun upstairs in my closet. I fitted an end into one leg of my football pants and the other end into the old golf bag that I lugged home from the dump. After that, Bud and Skip tried to catch me again, and this time they were out to get even, and get me. But I crawled along the mud under the corncrib and they never found me.

Then they limped on home.

Mama made me take an old bath that

night, and when I was all squeaky and clean, I hugged her very hard, whispering into her ear that it really *was* my gun. She laughed, and Papa laughed, saying they knew it was all the time. Maybe my mother just wanted to make sure I'd get good and even with Skip and Bud.

Then she put a soft white bandage on my knee; and Papa told me a Melvin Purvis story, with lots of shooting in it, the kind that really puts me to sleep. I tucked Fred, my Shirley Temple doll, into bed with me to show them how good I was and how fond I was of Aunt Augusta. After they turned my lamp down low, they left, so I had a chance to kiss Bill Dickey's picture. Then I asked Fred to hitch over a little to make area for my Junior G-man machine gun which I got up and got. I sure had a hanker for it. But just so my doll's feelings wouldn't get hurt, I hugged one arm around Mel, my gun, and the other around Fred.

Closing my eyes, I let my head sink in the pillow. When I grow up, I was thinking, it sure would be a tribulation as whether I'd be boss of the G-men or catcher for the Yanks. Well, I don't guess I'll do baseball on account I already got a Melvin Purvis machine gun instead of a catcher's mitt.

"God bless Melvin," I whispered, "and Bill Dickey, and a special God bless for Uncle Fred." Then I included Mom and Papa, and old Bud and Fat Face. When those two guys chase me, they couldn't even catch cold, but I reckon I'd forgive them and I didn't care a spit if they forgive me. And I even remembered Aunt Augusta, but what I was really blessing was the bee. Or rather the hornet.

And then, just as I dropped off to sleep, I thought I heard a big deep voice that I'd Sunday swear on a Baptist Bible was old John Dillinger say . . .

"Good night, Trig."